ALICE

Titles in Papercuts:

THE TRICK
KATE ORMAND

SCISSOR MAN
TIM COLLINS

QUEEN OF FLIES
TIM COLLINS

ALICE
DANNY PEARSON

THE SICKNESS
JACQUELINE RAYNER

A LITTLE SECRET
ANN EVANS

Badger Publishing Limited, Oldmedow Road, Hardwick Industrial Estate, King's Lynn PE30 4JJ

Telephone: 01438 791037

www.badgerlearning.co.uk

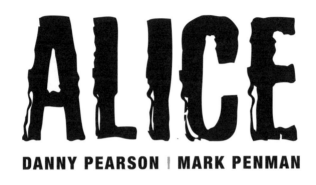

ALICE

DANNY PEARSON | MARK PENMAN

"Tomorrow will be the first day of the rest of your life."

Badger
LEARNING

Alice ISBN 978-1-78837-219-0

Text © Danny Pearson 2018
Complete work © Badger Publishing Limited 2018

Publisher: Susan Ross
Senior Editor: Danny Pearson
Editorial Coordinator: Claire Morgan
Copyeditor: Cheryl Lanyon
Designer: Bigtop Design Ltd
Illustration: Mark Penman

2 4 6 8 10 9 7 5 3 1

CHAPTER 1
THE STORM

The rain was beating hard against Alice's bedroom window. She could hear the howl of the wind raging over the music she was playing in her room.

She was trying to make a start on her assignment that needed to be in by the end of the week. Usually she would have finished the work days before but she was finding it hard to concentrate.

"Alice!" called her mother, Carol, from the bottom of the stairs. "Can I get you anything?"

"No Mum," she called back. "I'm fine thank you."

Her mum knew that something wasn't right with Alice lately, but she could hardly blame her. It had been hard since Alice's dad had left.

Alice had thought she had the perfect parents but that was all shattered after her dad left them for one of her mum's best friends. Worse yet, the now ex-best friend was a teacher at Alice's school — Miss Hart.

Alice had only heard rumours at first, whispers and messages between students, but it was now public knowledge that Miss Hart and her dad were together.

Kids at school had even taken photos of the happy couple meeting up outside the school entrance. Alice hated her dad for that. How could he be so selfish? He had destroyed her mum and now he was destroying her too.

Alice was never the most popular girl at school, but she was by no means at the bottom of the social pile. The stuff with her dad had now made sure that everyone was gossiping about her, which made her feel angry and alone. Only one of Alice's friends, Hattie, had stuck by her over the last few weeks. But even she was starting to talk to her less and less on the bus and between lessons. Hattie was drifting away and Alice knew it.

Alice tried to ignore the sound of the rain drumming on her window. She tried to focus on her assignment again. She needed to get it done. She had to show her dad that she didn't need him. That she would be fine on her own. She would pass her exams, get a good job and take her mum away from all of the mess that he had caused.

Ding, ding

Alice's phone sounded from the other side of her room. Hopefully it was Hattie with a message or funny video of a cat. That would cheer her up.

She picked up her phone and opened the message. It was from a private number and it had a picture attached which was loading. Alice knew what was

coming next. She had received ten more like this
one over the last few days. The picture loaded to
reveal her dad kissing Miss Hart.

Alice threw her phone on her bed and screamed.
When will they get bored of sending me these stupid photos?
she thought to herself. She wanted to move on.
To forget about the fact that her family was broken.

Lightning flashed outside her window. Something
caught Alice's eye. She briefly saw a shape outside
her window. Something was outside. She turned
off her music and stood there to listen.

The wind moaned and the rain beat harder
against the glass. Alice crept closer and closer.
Another flash lit up whatever it was outside her
window. Alice jumped backwards. There was no
doubt now that something was there.

The window was fogging up from the outside.
She could feel a nervous chill run down her spine
as she edged closer, but she couldn't help but

look. A flash of lightning lit up the shape by the window. It wasn't human. It was too small.

Thunder raged and another flash came seconds after. Alice was now close enough to see what was pressed up against the glass. She could make out a cat's face peering in — staring at her.

The drenched cat looked hard at Alice and began to paw against the glass. She had to do something. The cat was so soaked she could see streaks of skin poking through its wet, black fur. Its tail was curled round underneath its wet belly and its ears were hanging lifelessly by the sides of its head.

Alice lifted the window open and the cat darted in. The wind and rain lashed in too. She quickly shut the window and spun around to see her new guest, grabbing a towel as she turned.

The jet-black cat gave a full body shake and then sat there licking its paws and wiping its face. A puddle had already formed on the carpet around it. Alice bent down and wrapped the cat in her towel. She began to rub it up and down, collecting pools of water that were draining from the cat's inky fur.

"Hey," she whispered in the cat's direction. "What were you doing out there? You should be inside."

After a few minutes of drying off, the cat stopped licking and raised its head to meet Alice's gaze. She wondered if the cat belonged to someone. It looked far too clean and well-kept to be a stray. Alice then caught sight of a tiny name tag hanging from a black collar. She lifted it closer to study the tag. There was only one thing written on it — *Chester*.

"Chester," Alice said warmly. "That's a very handsome name for a very handsome cat."

Alice was now sitting cross-legged on her bedroom floor as her new guest was circling, occasionally brushing up against her and letting off a low purr as it moved. Alice ran her fingers through the now-dry cat's fur. It felt so soft and warm. She hadn't felt this relaxed in weeks.

The cat hopped into her lap and curled up in the gap between her knees. Alice pushed her back up against the end of the bed and sat there, watching the cat's chest rise up and down as a chorus of purring filled the room.

She then laid her head back and stared up at the posters and postcards on her ceiling. She could see deserts, jungles and snow all in one go. She dreamed of leaving and travelling the world. All the posters had come from magazines and the postcards were bought from antique shops. She loved reading the backs of them as they always had happy messages about people's travels. No one ever sent a postcard with bad news on the back.

Alice had always planned to travel after she had finished school, but all that had changed now of course. She knew it would be a while yet before she could leave her mum on her own. Alice's life, as well as her mum's, had been shattered. And with the distant dreams of travelling the world, and the soft sound of her new friend purring below, Alice slipped into sleep.

The storm outside passed and the late evening was calmly turning into night.

As the light of the moon shone through Alice's bedroom window, the cat looked up and smiled a wide, toothy smile. "This is the Alice I have been looking for."

CHAPTER 2
CHESTER

Alice sat bolt upright. Her left side had gone numb and she felt stiff. She couldn't figure out why she was on her bedroom floor but then everything came flooding back. Her assignment, the storm, and Chester!

"Chester!" she called out as she stood up. "Chester, are you still here?"

She ran round her room looking for any signs of the black cat.

"Alice, is everything OK?" her mum called out to her from the other bedroom.

"Yes, Mum," she answered. "Everything is… erm… fine."

"OK dear," her mum said. "Hurry up and get some breakfast. You don't want to be late for school."

Alice quickly scanned her room again for any sign of Chester. It was no good. He wasn't in her room any more.

Was he even real? Alice thought to herself. She then looked down at her feet and saw the wet towel that she had used to dry him with on the floor. Relieved that she hadn't been dreaming, Alice thought about looking downstairs quickly, before her mum made her way down. Frantically she ran down the stairs and started to check each room.

"Are you OK?" her mum asked again as she entered the kitchen. "You look a little flustered."

Alice caught her reflection in the kettle and

could see beads of sweat had started to collect on her forehead. "Yes I'm fine. I just didn't get much sleep."

This was, of course, a lie. It was one of the best nights' sleep Alice had had in weeks. Even if it was on the floor. She had a flashback of Chester purring, filling her room with positive energy. She had felt so relaxed.

"You're going to miss your bus if you don't hurry up," said her mum. "Grab some toast and get yourself off to school."

*

The fine rain was collecting on Alice's face as she waited for her bus. Yet again she had forgotten to put an umbrella in her bag and now she was paying for it. Her shoulder-length blonde hair was collecting tiny droplets of rain that were now dripping onto the back of her school blazer.

Her bus stop was the only one without a shelter.

She was the last student to be picked up on the way to school and the first to be dropped off. In the summer she was baked by the sun and in the winter she had to stand there in the freezing winds or, worse yet, sleet.

The bus turned the corner and stopped by the curb where she stood. The door opened and she was flooded by the noise and chaos of a busload of school children.

"Come on. Hurry up!" the bus driver shouted. "I'm running late."

She quickly climbed the steps onto the bus, where she stood looking for her friend Hattie. She usually saved Alice a seat in the middle of the bus which was an area reserved for people who weren't super-cool, but normal. Alice stood on her tip-toes. She could just make out the top of Hattie's head but she was towards the back in the popular crowd, sitting with someone else.

"Come on!" yelled the bus driver. "Take a seat so I can get going."

He was pointing at the seats directly behind him. Alice turned to see there were only two seats left and they were both at the very front.

She threw her bag in the rack above and slid down onto the seat. *Has Hattie cut all ties with me now?* she thought to herself. Hattie always used to save Alice a seat. She looked to see where Hattie was again, but as she turned she caught Hattie ducking behind a seat. It was clear that she didn't want Alice to see her that morning.

"Hey, Alice!" came a cry from the back of the bus.

She knew who it was and turned back round in her seat to face the front, trying to ignore the call.

"Oi! Loser," came another cry from the back. "Look at us when we're talking to you."

Alice didn't turn. She knew if she did then insults would be thrown directly at her face. Alice preferred that they were given to her back, that way they didn't seem to hurt as much.

The twins from her class ruled the back of the bus. They were a horrible pair, but they were the prettiest girls in school or, at least, that's what most people thought anyway.

"I heard your dad was out again with Miss Hart last night!" Dee, the smaller of the twins, shouted out towards the front of the bus.

Donna, the taller twin, followed up with, "I wonder if your dad has a thing for teachers. Best warn the rest of them before parents' evening."

That was it. Donna had delivered the early-morning killer blow. The bus erupted into laughter.

Alice sat there alone, tightening her fists so hard that her nails were digging into her palms. She couldn't say anything back. She knew she would be laughing too if they had made the same joke about someone else's parent. And now even Hattie, her best friend, had ditched her. She had nobody.

"Quiet, you lot!" shouted the moody bus driver. "I'm trying to concentrate!"

Alice sat back and placed her headphones around her head. She pressed her head up against the glass and closed her eyes. She could feel the bus shudder down the road as she dreamed of lying on a warm, sunny beach, a million miles away from the damp school bus.

Alice slowly opened her eyes, lost in her music, and looked out of the rain-smeared window. Something was watching her from a branch on the other side of the road. She caught a quick glimpse, locking eyes with the familiar creature.

"Chester," Alice whispered to herself.

CHAPTER 3
SLEEP

Dee and Donna were relentless. They made cheap comments during every lesson they shared with Alice, which spilled out into morning break and lunch. More photos of Miss Hart and her dad had surfaced and were doing the rounds at school. But the most crushing one was saved for when she got back on the bus after school.

Laughter filled the back seats and, after a tidal wave of message alerts and giggles, the picture message finally reached Alice's phone.

Someone had got a picture from the internet of a teacher spanking a man. Of course someone had then taken the time to paste Alice's dad's face on the man and Miss Hart's face on the teacher.

"Who did this?" Alice screamed as she stood up to face the busload of laughing students.

The bus fell silent for a few seconds as everyone looked to the twins on the back seat.

"Who did what?" asked Dee.

"This!" Alice said as she held up her phone, showing the altered photo.

"Looks pretty real to me," laughed Donna. "Is it one from the family album?"

A wave of laughter filled the bus again. Alice could see that Hattie was squirming in her seat. She wasn't laughing. She just sat there looking at the floor, unable to look at Alice.

"Sit down! Sit down now!" shouted the bus driver.

Alice sat back down. Tears were forming in the corners of her eyes but she didn't want anyone to see her get upset.

As soon as the bus pulled up to her stop she grabbed her bag and ran home through the pouring rain. She raced upstairs to her room, threw her bag on the floor and jumped on her bed. That's when she buried her face in her pillow and began to cry.

Through her sobbing Alice heard a tapping sound. She looked over at her door. Her mum wouldn't be back from work this early. Then she heard the tapping again. She turned and looked towards her bedroom window.

"Chester!" she cried. "You silly cat. What are you doing outside in this rain again?"

She raced over to the window and let the soggy feline in. After the awful day she'd had she was glad to share his calming company again. Just like before, he scurried quickly to the middle of the room and gave himself a shake.

"Thank you, Alice," he said. "I was getting soaked out there waiting for you."

Alice froze. Clutching a towel in one hand.

"Be a good girl and pass me that towel," Chester said, pointing with his paw.

Alice bent down on one knee and handed the black cat the dry towel. She kneeled there studying him for a moment, trying to choose her next words carefully.

"You talk?" she blurted out. She realised that it didn't sound like the most intelligent question she could have started with.

"It would seem that way," he answered as he rattled the corner of the towel around in his right ear.

Alice rocked backwards and sat down on the floor.

"This can't be happening."

"What was that, my dear?" asked the cat.

Alice looked up to face him. "You. This. Why are you talking?"

"Would you prefer it if I didn't?" asked Chester.

"No," Alice quickly replied. "I mean, this is amazing but… why can I understand you?"

"Because I am speaking English," Chester said with a smile.

Alice raised an eyebrow. "That's not what I meant and you know it."

Chester threw the damp towel onto a chair and padded over to her.

"Well I couldn't help but notice that you looked a little unhappy," he said as he sat on his back legs.

"That's true," Alice said looking down at the floor. "Everyone at school hates me. Nothing has been the same since my…"

"Since your dad ran away with one of your teachers," interrupted Chester. "Yes, I know all about that."

"You do?" asked Alice as she slowly raised her head to look at the black cat sitting in front of her.

"I do indeed, Alice. A girl as special as you shouldn't be worrying herself with such nonsense," he said.

"Ha! Special," Alice snorted. "I am anything but special."

Chester leaped onto the bed. He was now staring deep into Alice's eyes. "Oh, but you are Alice. You are remarkable."

Alice began to feel sleepy. The more she looked into Chester's eyes, the more her own eyes wanted to close.

"What… what do you mean, remarkable?" asked Alice with a yawn.

"Don't you worry about that now," said Chester. He looked deeper into Alice's eyes. "The most important thing is that I have found you."

He began to purr gently. The soft sound filled the room again and Alice could feel herself drifting off to sleep.

"Sleep, my precious Alice," he whispered as a wide, fanged grin spread across his face. "Tomorrow will be the first day of the rest of your life."

CHAPTER 4
RELAX

Knock, knock.

Alice woke to find that she was no longer on the floor but in her bed.

"Chester?" she called out. "Is that you?"

Her mum came crashing into her room and started to scurry round, picking up Alice's dirty clothes from the floor.

"Chester? Who is Chester?" her mum asked.

Alice looked around her room searching for him. She spotted him sitting up at her desk. He raised a paw to his lips, indicating for Alice to keep quiet.

She glanced over at him and then back at her mum. "Oh, nothing, Mum. Sorry. I was having a dream."

Her mum looked over at her with a smile on her face. "A dream about a Chester? Is Chester a boy you fancy from school?"

"No, Mum," sighed Alice.

"Sure, sure," her mum said with a wink. "Your secret little crush is safe with me."

She carried on picking up Alice's clothes from the floor. "I'm so sorry I was late back last night. I crept up here to check on you but you were already asleep. I hope you found time to cook yourself some dinner last night?"

"Yeah, I did, Mum," lied Alice.

"Good," her mum said. "Now hurry up and get changed. You don't want to be late for school… or Chester."

Her mum closed the door behind her and Alice turned to look over at the black cat again.

"I can't believe she didn't see you," Alice said with relief. "I would have been grounded for a month if she had seen you here."

Chester leaped down and headed over to where Alice was lying. His fur seemed to be darker, even darker than jet-black, and spikier. His eyes no longer looked soft, and they now had a red tint to them.

"I wouldn't worry about that," he said with a smile. "She would never be able to see me and we don't want people thinking you're crazy and talking to yourself."

Alice wiped the sleep from the corners of her eyes. "What do you mean by that?"

"Only someone of your rare talent has earned the right to see my kind."

"Your kind?" Alice said. "But you're just a cat. Well, a talking cat, but still a cat. Tell me what you mean."

"It is no accident that we should meet, Alice," said Chester.

His smile had turned into something more menacing. The fur running down his spine was standing on edge and his claws were growing longer.

"Chester! You're scaring me," said Alice in a cracked voice.

"Don't be scared, Alice," he said as his eyes shone. "I told you yesterday that tomorrow would be the first day of the rest of your life. And now, here we are."

Alice jumped from her bed, threw on her school shirt, and headed to the door. Chester raised a paw and hissed. With a short, sharp click the door locked.

"Wait, Alice!" he called. "If you leave now you will never know what you are truly capable of."

"Chester — you look different and you're scaring me," said Alice. "I don't know who you think I am but you need to let me go!"

The black creature crawled across to the end of Alice's bed. "Don't be afraid. I can show you other worlds. The more you believe, the more you will see things for what they are."

Alice sank to the floor. "I don't… I don't know what you're trying to tell me."

"Relax, my dear Alice," he said softly. "You have a gift. You just haven't unlocked it yet."

"What gift?" asked Alice. "If it's the gift of turning into a total loser, a screw-up, then yes, I *am* the one you're looking for!"

"This business with your dad, with school and your so-called friends, is so beneath you," Chester said as he edged closer to Alice.

He studied his new claws and looked at Alice. "You have the power to travel to other worlds, new dimensions. Time means nothing to you."

Alice started to shake. "I still don't understand."

Chester carried on inching closer to her. "It is my job to find people with your gift. You don't know it yet but inside you lies an amazing power. Only once every few hundred years does such a talent appear," he said. "What you do with it is up to you. Now, look at me so I can unlock your true potential."

She looked up to see Chester's eyes glowing bright red. Her head felt light again and the room was slowly turning.

"But… but why me?" she asked.

Chester grinned; he now had a mouth full of razor-sharp fangs. "The question you should ask, Alice, is *why not you*?"

Alice felt her body go limp and she slowly settled to the floor. The question *Why not you?* echoed inside her head as her eyes closed.

CHAPTER 5
POWER

Ding, ding.

Alice's phone sounded again. She stood
up from the floor and shuffled to her phone.
She wondered how long she had been asleep.
And Chester — where was Chester?

She picked up her phone and saw that it was
almost lunchtime and that she had been out cold
for hours. She opened up the message. It was
from a private number again and it had another
picture attached.

The message read: *Shame you couldn't make it to school
today. You're missing out on so much xXx*

Attached was another edited picture of her dad and Miss Hart.

"Arghhh! Stop it!" raged Alice.

Her phone cracked and then burst into flames. Alice screamed and threw it to the floor, stamping on it to smother the flames.

"You have to be more careful," came a familiar voice from under her bed.

"Chester? Is that you?" Alice said as she bent down to look. "Was… was that you who did that to my phone?"

Out of the shadows Alice could see two flaming red eyes appear, followed by a white streak of fangs. "No Alice. That was all you."

"What have you done to me?" she cried.

"Me?" said Chester. "I have merely unlocked your true potential. Your true power. It is all you from here on in."

"What are you saying?" screamed Alice.

Chester crept out from the shadows and pounced onto her bed. His handsome face had now twisted into something far more monstrous. His eyes burned red and his voice was more sinister. But Alice was not afraid. She felt like she was finally seeing the real beast she had invited in on the first night they met.

"Alice, you can go anywhere you like. Do anything you like. You have the power to destroy and to create. You can control objects, living things, even time itself. You can now choose any road you wish to go down."

"Which road do I take?" Alice asked the cat, who was sitting on her bed.

The cat asked, "Where do you want to go?"

"I don't know," Alice answered.

"Then," said the cat, "it really doesn't matter, does it?"

"This is crazy. What am I supposed to do with this gift?"

Chester lifted his face to meet hers. "That, my dear, is up to you. I was only sent here to help you unlock your powers. I can only show you how."

Alice looked up at the ceiling. She gazed over the posters and postcards. She had always dreamed of deserts, jungles and of white, sandy beaches. She dreamed once again of leaving her broken life and travelling the world.

"Can I really go anywhere I like? Anytime I like?"

"Yes, Alice. You can do all that and more," Chester said with a fang-filled grin. "But I sense you want to clear up some unfinished business first?"

Alice snapped her head back down and looked over at the burnt remains of her phone. Her eyes began to shine red too. A grin now spread across her face. "If you say I can really do all of those things then I think I know where I want to start."

"Excellent!" laughed Chester. "Then let's begin."

Alice closed her eyes as a flash of red light washed over her.

CHAPTER 6
ROADS

The red light disappeared and Alice opened her eyes again. She was now standing at the gates of her school.

"That was intense!" she said.

"You are a natural," whispered Chester into her left ear.

He was perched on top of Alice's shoulders. She could feel his sharp claws dig into her skin through her blazer, but she felt no pain.

Chester looked straight ahead at the school.

"So you can go anywhere, anytime, in the entire universe, and you decide to come here. Is this where your unfinished business waits?"

"It is," Alice said turning to him.

"Are we here to pay anyone in particular a visit?"

"Yes," smiled Alice. "But I want to say hello to a couple of people before I deal with her."

Alice made her way through the school gates and up towards the entrance.

She focused on the doors which flung open with just a thought.

It was after lunch and everyone was in their classrooms. Alice could feel the heartbeats of every single student and teacher in the school. She could hear the scratching of pens on paper, the buzzing of electricity from the computers, and the hands move on every clock in the building. She felt more alive than she had ever felt before.

"Focus," whispered Chester. "Focus on the prize you are after."

Alice shut her eyes again and listened. She could hear students laughing. Teachers teaching, and then…

"Upstairs. Room 31b," she said as a fresh smile crept across her face.

*

"This is so boring," sighed Dee, who was sitting behind a desk at the back of the classroom. "Double Maths. It's enough to send me to sleep."

"This should wake you up," laughed Donna. "I managed to make up another picture of Miss Hart and Alice's dad on the computer in Business Studies this morning. Check it out."

"Ha! That. Is. Hilarious," laughed Dee.

"Girls! No talking at the back, please," shouted

their teacher, Mr King. "Donna, is that a phone I see there? You know the rules — bring it here."

"But, Sir," whined Donna.

"'But, Sir' nothing. Give it to me now. I will keep hold of it and you can collect it at the end of school."

Donna stood up from her desk and marched towards the front of the class. Out of the corner of her eye she caught a figure staring at her from outside the classroom door.

"Alice?"

Mr King turned to see what Donna was looking at. He could see Alice standing there with her eyes fixed on Donna.

He strode over to the door and wrenched it open. "Alice. What are you doing out of class?"

She turned her gaze to Mr King, her eyes buzzed with a red tint. "Take a seat, Sir. This has nothing to do with you. It's them I want."

The whole class gasped as they saw Mr King fly across the front of the room and into a chair behind his desk. Alice had used her new-found powers to pin him to his seat.

"What are you doing, you freak?" shouted Donna.

Alice held out her hand and the phone flew out of Donna's hand. The phone hovered in front of Alice and she began to scroll through the photos on it.

"Oi, that's mine!" screamed Donna. "Give it back."

Alice could see photos of her dad and Miss Hart. She could also see private conversations and messages going back and forth between the sisters over many months.

Alice flicked her eyes back to Donna. "Been busy I see."

"Yeah. So?" snorted Donna.

Alice could feel her eyes burn brighter as Chester dug his claws deeper into her shoulders.

"You and your sister used to cause me so much pain. You and your pathetic pictures. But it ends now. Today everyone will see how messed up you two really are."

With a flick of Alice's head Donna's phone began to glow. Followed by a chorus of messaging alerts from other students' phones. Frantically everyone in the class searched for their phones and one-by-one they opened them. Streams of past conversations were being sent round the class. Horrible messages going back and forth between Donna and Dee were now out in the open for everyone to see.

Dee opened her phone to see what had been sent. "Donna. You need to see this."

Donna ran over to peer at the phone. The blood drained from her face as she scanned everything that was being sent out to her fellow classmates.

Two girls sitting near the twins saw messages going back and forth between Dee, Donna and the girls' boyfriends. Private conversations and photos. They turned and glared at the cowering sisters.

"It wasn't us," cried Donna.

Dee pleaded with the class. "Can't you see that Alice has made all of this up?"

"Why are you sending my boyfriend photos?" asked one of the girls from the desk in front of them.

"We… we aren't," whimpered Donna.

The girl grabbed a chunk of Donna's hair. "Why are you sending my boyfriend photos?"

"Girls! Girls!" cried Mr King from his seat that he was still rooted to. "Break it up, now!"

Another girl jumped over the desk and smacked Dee hard in the face. The class erupted into chaos.

Alice smiled over at the twin sisters. "Good luck trying to explain all of that."

She took one last look at the madness in front of her, turned, and walked out of the classroom. Alice then calmly climbed down the stairs and made her way over to another classroom. She peered through the glass and locked eyes with who she had really come for. With a surge of energy the door flung open and the class screamed as the glass in the door shattered.

"Miss Hart!" she called as her eyes shone red.

"Alice!" cried Miss Hart. "What is the meaning of this?"

Alice tilted her head to one side and Miss Hart was lifted from the ground. The students parted in a rush of yells and screams as Miss Hart flew across the classroom and was pinned against the back wall.

"What's happening to me?" Miss Hart cried. "Someone, please help me!"

Two students ran to help her down, but Alice pushed them back using her mind. She froze the entire class in their seats. No one could escape.

"If anyone is squeamish," announced Alice in a calm tone, "then I suggest you close your eyes."

"Oh, this is going to be fun," laughed the monster perched on her shoulders.

"Alice! What are you doing?" Miss Hart cried as she struggled against the wall. "If this is about your father then I'm sorry. I never meant to hurt you or your mum. It just happened."

"It just happened?" questioned Alice. "Nothing just happens. You knew he was married to your best friend, my mum, Carol. You chose to go down that road."

"I know. But… but… we're in love," Miss Hart said with tears rolling down her face.

Alice smiled to reveal her teeth, which now had sharp points to them. "Ha! I'm sure you are.

But I want to give you and Daddy a permanent reminder of the pain you have caused my mum and me."

Alice lifted her right hand and began to write in mid-air.

"Arghhh! What are you doing?" screamed Miss Hart. "Alice, stop!"

The letter C was being scratched into Miss Hart's forehead. Chester's eyes burned brighter with every wave of Alice's hand.

Blood wept from the fresh wounds appearing on the teacher's skin. A horrific cry of pain rang out with every mark made. Alice could feel Chester's claws dig deeper into her shoulders as she flicked her wrists in the air like a mad conductor.

After the *C* followed an *A*, then an *R*, and then an *O*. This was finally followed with an *L*.

"Perfect," Alice said with a nod. "Just so you know, I have also just made the same marks on my dad's forehead. Now you can both be reminded of the pain you caused my mum every time you look at each other. Goodbye, Miss Hart."

Alice turned and left the classroom. The students were still pinned to their seats, their mouths forced shut, with tears streaming from their eyes as Miss Hart collapsed from the wall and fell into a sobbing heap.

Chester looked back at the broken teacher on the floor. "Nice touch, Alice. I can see you are going to be lots of fun."

Alice caught her own reflection in a window. She could see the feline monster, who had once been so handsome, on her shoulders. But she had changed too. "I feel so alive Chester. With this new power I can feel and hear so many places; connect to so many different worlds and times."

Her eyes were like Chester's, burning red, and her skin crawled with electricity.

Teachers and students, who had heard Miss Hart's blood-curdling cries, were flooding out of their rooms and into the corridor. They all stood back from Alice, staring at her in terror. She could see her so-called best friend, Hattie, peering out from one of the classrooms with tears of fear forming in her eyes.

Chester slowly curled his tail around Alice's neck. "Where do you wish to go now, Alice?"

She took one last look at her reflection; one last look at what she had become, and smiled. "I'm done with this place. This time," she said as her tongue rolled over a row of fresh, sharp teeth.

Her eyes rolled back in their sockets and a bright red light filled the corridor.

"It's time to take you and my mum away from here. For good."

THE END

ABOUT THE AUTHOR

Danny Pearson lives in 'The Shire', near London, England. He is very much a child of the 80s.

He was brought up on a diet of unusual cartoons and movies involving things changing into other things, or adventures set to cheap keyboard soundtracks. Mobile phones were as big as a shed and the internet was still in black and white.

ABOUT THE ARTIST

Mark Penman is a freelance illustrator, comic book artist and art lecturer hailing from the rainy North East of England. When not writing and drawing his own comics Mark enjoys reading horror and fantasy books and indulging in his passion for history. This passion for bygone times has led Mark to begin practising medieval longsword combat in the hope he may be whisked away to a magical kingdom where he will save it from an impending evil. Well, we all gotta daydream right?